By Rose & Frank Winn

The Adventures of Rose Bud

Illustrated by usillustrations.com

2023

Dedicated to my mother and Rose's Nana.
A woman who had many special gifts and
will always be our biggest fan.

This is the first of several books, about a very special ladybug. Her name is Rose Bud.

Born 1 of 21 ladybugs, she was born with a rose over her heart. Her mother instantly called her Rose Bud, because she was much too beautiful to be just another ladybug.

Soon after her birth, Rose Bud asks about her Dad. Her mother explained that one winter day he went off in search of food and never returned.

Rose Bud is determined to find her Dad, which ends up taking her on many exciting adventures.
Little does she realize that the rose over her heart is not only beautiful but has a special power.

A power that can sometimes change bad to good Rose Bud's underlying message to everyone is, "Let's be friends".

Rose Bud is Born

This is the first of several books, about a very special ladybug. Her name is Rose Bud.

Born 1 of 21 ladybugs, she was born with a rose over her heart. Her mother instantly called her Rose Bud, because she was much too beautiful to be just another ladybug.

Soon after her birth, Rose Bud asks about her Dad. Her mother explained that one winter day he went off in search of food and never returned.

Rose Bud is determined to find her Dad, which ends up taking her on many exciting adventures.
Little does she realize that the rose over her heart is not only beautiful but has a special power.

A power that can sometimes change bad to good Rose Bud's underlying message to everyone is, "Let's be friends".

Once upon a time in a land far away
there was a tiny village.

Everyone was busy preparing for the long-awaited
arrival of Mrs. Eleanor's loveliness of ladybugs.

HONEY
Raisins
HONEY

Baskets of lettuce, jars of honey, and
bushels of raisins were being gathered
for the long-awaited arrival.

Raisins

"We must hurry," cried Katie. "We don't want to
miss a thing!"

"Relax," said Blu. "We have waited a long time for this magical day and a few more moments won't matter."

"That's easy for you to say," Squeaky cried!
"Not all of us have wings and can fly!"

"Stop bickering," stomped Coco. "We need to stop talking and start hopping!"

"Yeah," snarled Nicky. "Let's get moving!
It's time to turn on paw power!"

Mrs. Eleanor lived on the side of a hill,
in a beautiful green leaf house.

Everyone gathered outside Mrs. Eleanor's home ...... anxiously awaiting the arrival of the newborn ladybugs

Tic Toc, Tic Toc.......
Finally, the clock struck dawn!

18

At last, Coco yelled!

"They're here! They're here"!
"The Lady bunnies are here"!
"Oops, I mean the ladybugs are here"!!

Everyone jumped for joy!!

Mrs. Eleanor gave birth to 21 beautiful baby ladybugs.
10 boys and 11 girls!!!

Even amongst all the excitement,
Blu could tell something was wrong.

"What's up, Coco?" Blu asked.
"You look like you've just seen a ghost?"

It's ... It's one of the ladybugs, Coco stuttered.

One of the girls La... La... ladybugs is different!

"What do you mean, different?" Blu asked, confused.
"Does the ladybug have all of her spots?"
"Does she have six legs?"

"Does she have an antenna?"
"What is different?" Blu begged.

"Yes, she has her spots!"
"Yes, she has six legs!"
"Yes, she has an antenna, but something's not right,"
Snapped Coco.

"One of the babies was born with a red rose
over her heart," Coco explained.
Blu looked at Coco confused and surprised.

Meanwhile, everyone was celebrating
with the newborn ladybugs.

It wasn't until "Big mouth," Bitsy let out a gasp!

"Look, look everyone! One of the ladybugs has a rose
over her heart!"

"Now, now, everyone, no need to make a fuss."

Mrs. Eleanor slowly picked up her little ladybug and
looked at her and gave a loving smile.
"You are a beautiful little ladybug, and it appears
you have been born with a very special gift."

Mrs. Eleanor announced with excitement, "I'm going to call you my little Rose Bud."

34

Time passed and everyone had fun playing with
the family of ladybugs.

FURY TAILS   LADYBUGS
00 : 08

Daily routines included family dinners...

... and plenty of bedtime stories

One day, while playing a game of "Ring around
the Rose Bud,"
Rose Bud asked her mother about her dad.

"Momma," Rose Bud asked. "Why have I never
seen my Daddy?"

Mrs. Eleanor paused for a second... then explained to Rose Bud that her father had gone off one winter in search of food but never returned.

Rose Bud's eyes began to tear, and she started to cry.

She knew instantly what she must do.

The next day, Rose Bud gathered all her friends together and explained to them her plans to go and find her dad.

Everyone gathered to bid farewell to Rose Bud as she set sail on her first Adventure.

Let's Be Friends

www.ingramcontent.com/pod-product-compliance
Lightning Source LLC
Chambersburg PA
CBHW041412300726
48978CB00002B/64